IMAGINE THAT™

Licensed exclusively to Imagine That Publishing Ltd
Tide Mill Way, Woodbridge, Suffolk, IP12 1AP, UK
www.imaginethat.com
Copyright © 2020 Imagine That Group Ltd
All rights reserved
2 4 6 8 9 7 5 3
Manufactured in China

Written by Isadora Rose
Illustrated by Alex Willmore

ISBN 978-1-78958-485-1

A catalogue record for this book is available from the British Library

The Sound of MOO-SIC!

MOO!
MOO!
MOO!

Written by Isadora Rose
Illustrated by Alex Willmore

Connor Cow loved to sing.

He sang all day long. In fact, the only time that he wasn't singing was when he was fast asleep!

One day, Connor grew tired of singing on his own.

'I'm going to sing for my friends,' said Connor, happily.

Not far away, Connor spotted Olivia Owl hurrying to her treetop home in the woods.

'I'll sing for Olivia,' thought Connor, excitedly.

'Moo! Moo! Moo!' sang Connor at the top of his voice.

'Stop it!' yelled Olivia. 'I've been out all night and I want to go to sleep. Go and sing somewhere else, please!'

'Moo!' said Connor.

Walking through the woods,
Connor came to a
small clearing.

'This looks like a theatre,'
he chuckled. 'I'll put on a
special show for Dora Deer!'

'Moo! Moo! Moo!' sang Connor, louder than ever before.

But Dora didn't stay to listen. The noise was so loud it scared her away!

'Moo!' said Connor.

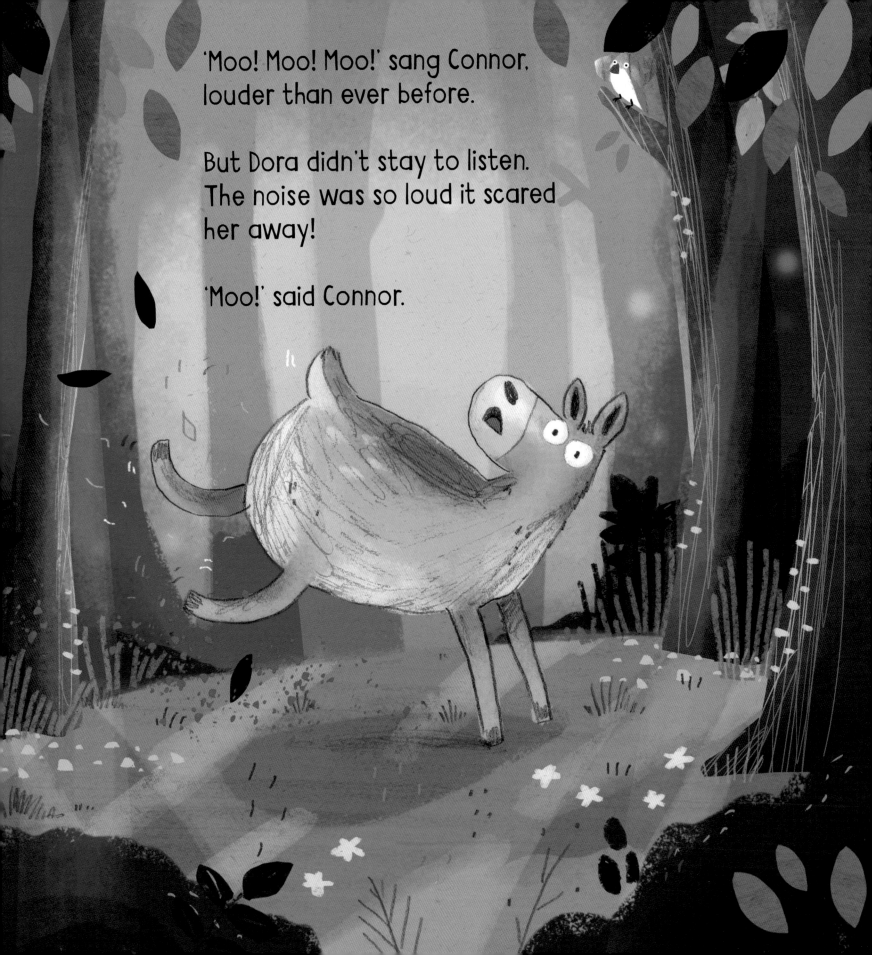

Natalie Nightingale was resting in a tree at the edge of the woods.

'Moo! Moo! Moo!' began Connor, but Natalie held her wings to her ears.

'Please don't sing for me,' she said ...

CHIRP!
CHIRRUP!
CHEEP!

'... let me sing for you!
Birds have a much
sweeter voice. Listen!'

Then Natalie Nightingale
filled the air with
beautiful birdsong.

'Moo!' said Connor.

'Nobody wants me to sing,'
sighed Connor, sadly.

Connor was just about to
go home when he heard a
commotion coming from
just up ahead.

Connor followed the noise and was amazed to discover a field that was filled with cows just like him. Best of all, the cows were all singing!

'Come and make moo-sic with us!' said the cows when they spied Connor. 'We love singing!'

Connor had never been so happy!
'Now I'm part of a choir!' he chuckled.